AF379410

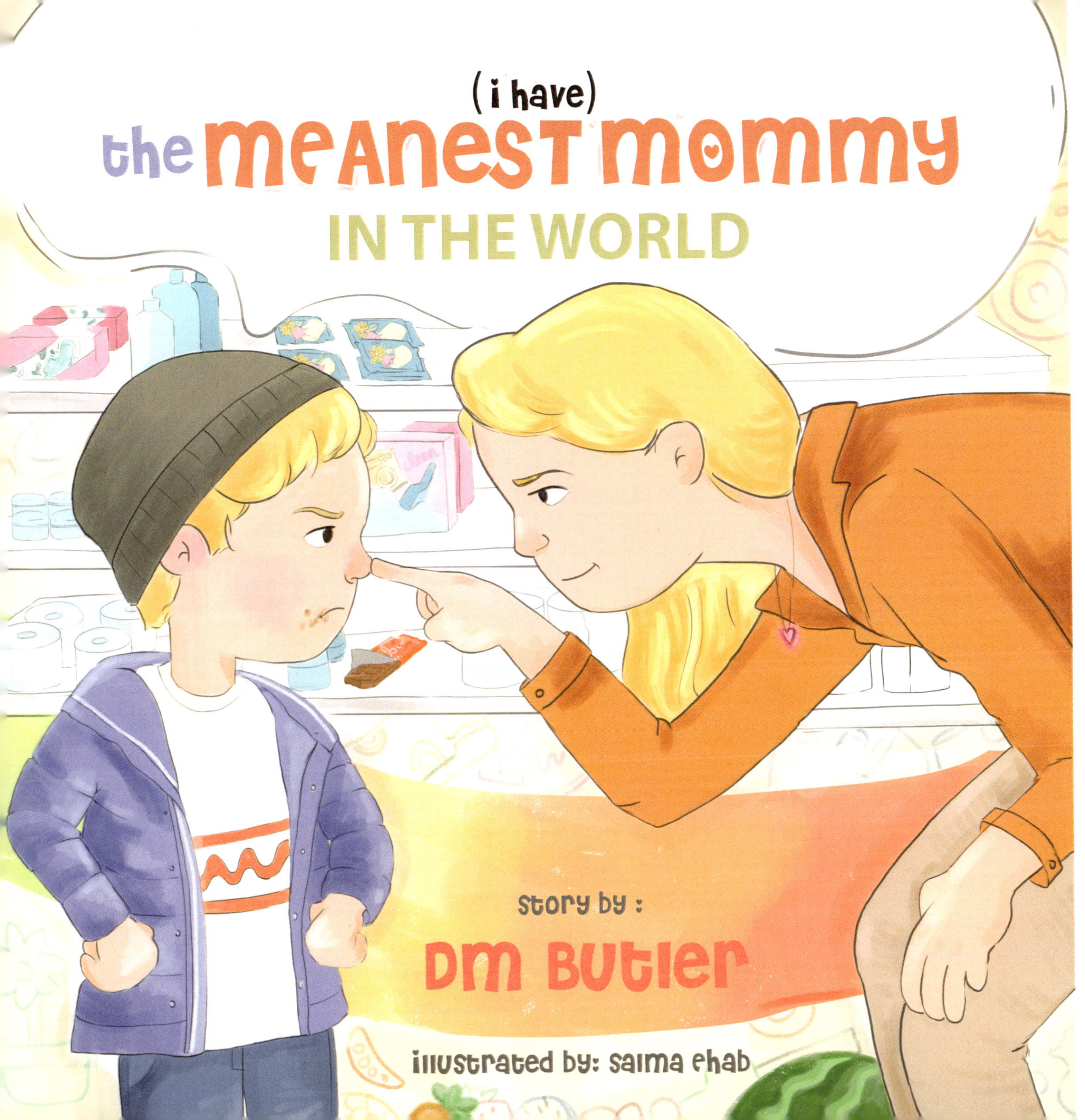

(i have)
the MEANEST mommy
IN THE WORLD
story by :
DM Butler
illustrated by: saima ehab

The Meanest Mommy
is part of the DMB DeLIGHTful Development collection.

Illustrated by Salma Ehab
Copyright© 2024

I have the
Meanest Mommy

She makes me brush my hair

and every single morning
put on clean fresh underwear

Then when I'm dressed and ready
to finally have some fun
she makes me stop
and brush my teeth

Every. Single. One.

My mommy says it's not okay
to eat fruit snacks all the time
but I'm not afraid of a tummyache
when there is lemon–lime

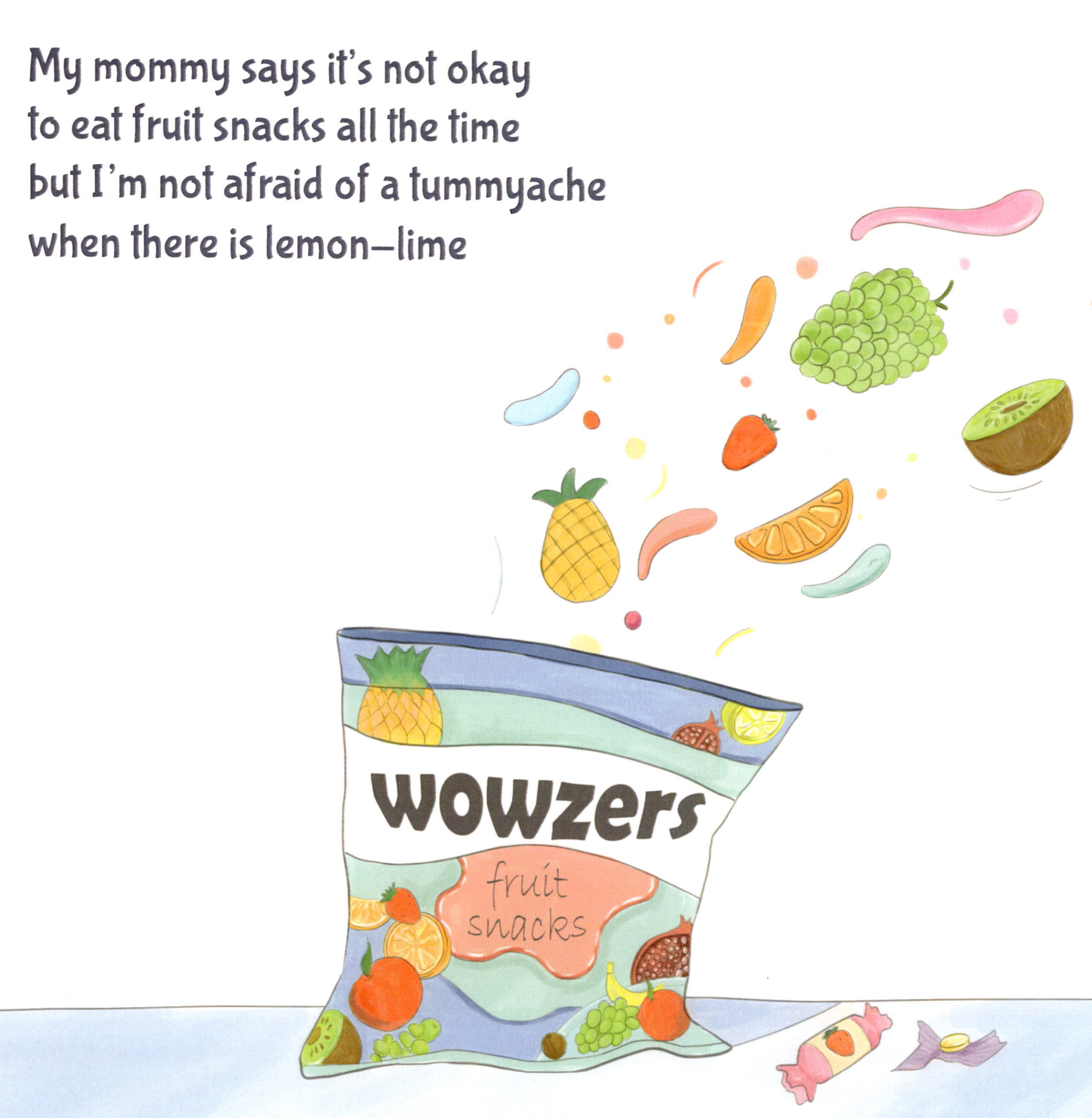

and strawberry and orange
yummy grape and tangerine
in chocolate sauce if I were boss
and my mommy weren't so mean

If my mommy used MY grocery list
our cart would be filled with treats

maybe one bunch
of carrots or grapes ...
all that healthy stuff she eats

I would not make mommy blow
on her soup just because it's hot

or zip her coat to stay warm outside
pinky swear that I would not

Every time I get a sniffle
she makes me rest all day

First place
Diesel - wee

I sleep all night
so it's not alright
that she won't just let me play

I do not cross the street alone
she makes me hold her hand
I just can not get through to her
why won't she understand

I tell you I have the meanest mommy
every word of this is true
She makes me wash my hands with soap
when I make a pee or poo

On top of that I know my room
has to be the cleanest
of any kid in the whole wide world
because my mom is the meanest

My grandma says my mommy wants
what's best for me and so
I have to do the things she says
until I'm old enough, ya know

to have a kid and if I do

I won't make them do a thing

But then how will I keep them healthy ...

and warm ...

and safe ...

and clean

I suppose i'll make them just as mad
as I get once in a while

and when they shout

I'll give them an extra hug
(like my mom does)

and an extra mommy smile

About the author:

DM Butler is an American author, and still the meanest mommy to three grown children who inspire stories that speak to the experiences, emotions, and questions shared by all of us at every stage of life, but from a particular point of view when walking through all of life's "firsts" with so much to consider: fear, loss, values, responsibilities, and love in all its beautiful forms.

Write to DM Butler at
dmbutlerwrites@gmail.com